GUERNSEY MEMORIAL LIBRARY
DISCARD
A 0 00 04 0099048 7

King Midas

Published 1990
Printed in the United States of America

Library of Congress Cataloging-in-Publication Data
Newby, Robert, 1932–
King Midas.

Summary: Presents the classic tale of the king who wished that everything he touched would turn to gold. Line drawings depict selected sentences in American Sign Language.
1. Midas—Juvenile literature. 2. Sign language—Juvenile literature. [1. Midas. 2. Mythology, Greek. 3. Sign language] I. Majewski, Dawn, ill. II. Cozzolino, Sandra, ill. III. Hawthorne, Nathaniel, 1804–1864. King Midas and the golden touch. IV. Title.
BL820.M55N48 1990 398.22 90-4908
ISBN 0-930323-75-0 (lib. bdg.)

Gallaudet University Press
800 Florida Ave. N.E.
Washington, DC 20002

FOREST HOUSE ™

School & Library Edition

KING MIDAS

With Selected Sentences in American Sign Language

Nathaniel Hawthorne

Adaptation and Art Direction by Robert Newby

Illustrations by Dawn Majewski

Line Drawings by Sandra Cozzolino

Kendall Green Publications
Gallaudet University Press
Washington, D.C.

The Manual Alphabet

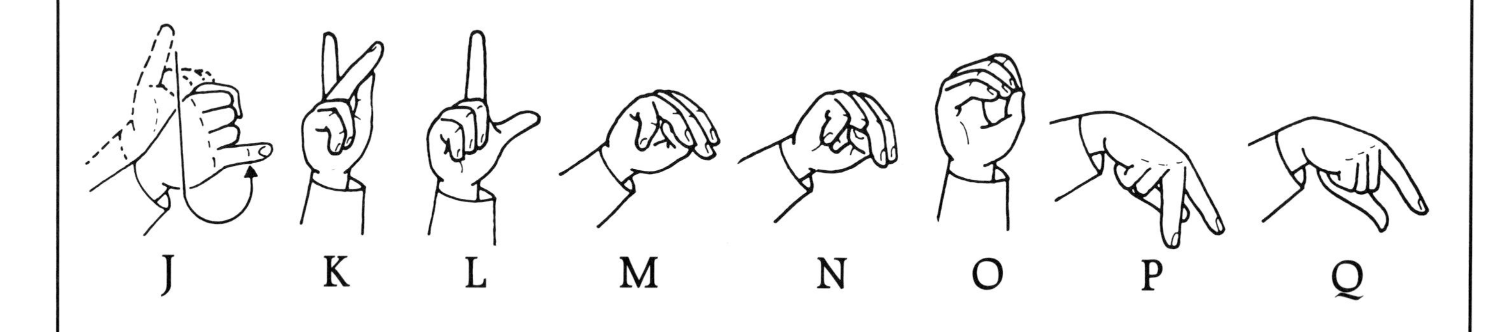

Numbers

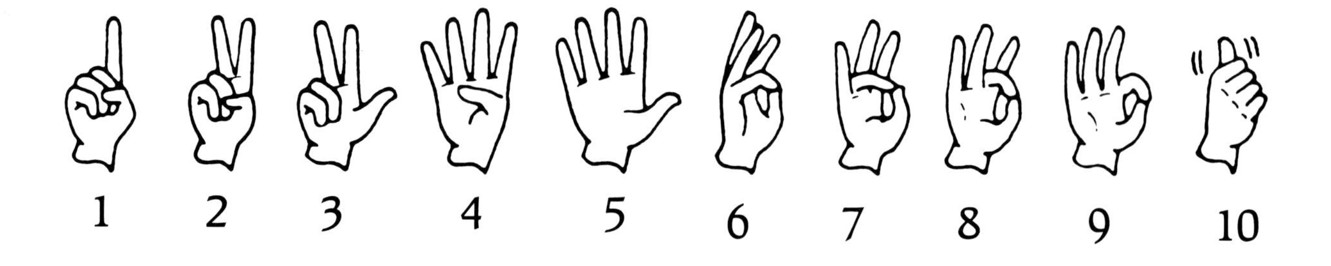

INTRODUCTION

American Sign Language, called ASL, is a fun and exciting language! Because deaf people cannot hear spoken language, some learn ASL to communicate with other deaf people and with hearing people who know sign. ASL is a language, like English, Spanish, or French. Signs are used like words are used in spoken languages. Sentences in ASL use signs in a different order than words are used in English, or Spanish, or French.

Some ASL signs can't be translated into English, nor can some English words be translated into signs. English words that can't be signed are spelled using the fingers of one hand. This is called *fingerspelling*; the hand forms the letters of the *manual alphabet*. By looking at the chart on the opposite page, you can tell that some of the letters in the manual alphabet look like written letters. Numbers are signed using the *manual numbers*.

Some signs are made using one hand and some are made using two hands. Usually people use the hand that they write and eat with to sign the one-handed signs and to fingerspell. When making two-handed signs, use the hand you write with to make the main movement. The signs in this book are drawn for right-handed people. If you are left-handed, reverse the signs.

Using your face and body to help express what you are signing is an important part of ASL. Sometimes, the face expresses as much information as the signs. If deaf people are signing *love*, a big smile lights up their faces. Or if they are signing *angry*, a frown crosses their faces. Quite often, when people ask a question in English, their faces change. Their eyebrows move up, their eyes open wide, and their foreheads crinkle. Deaf people do the same thing, but to a greater degree, because face and body movements are part of ASL. And sometimes the signer will draw a question mark in the air at the end of the question.

In ASL, you can show the shape of something by using your hands to shape the object that you are describing. The shapes of bottles—tall and narrow, short and fat—can be shown in this way. Use your left hand as a base and "draw" the shape of the bottle with your entire right hand—or you can use both hands. You can tell by the sign how the bottle in the story is shaped.

Signs are made using *handshapes*. Some handshapes use the letters from the manual alphabet or the manual numbers, which you can see on the opposite page. There are other special handshapes, too. The special handshapes you will see in *King Midas* are shown below, illustrated by a sign in the story.

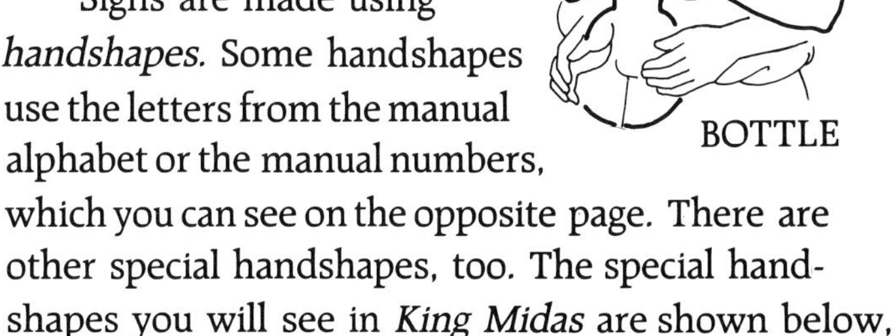

BOTTLE

Claw: WISH

Flat O: MORE

Bent V: SIT

Curved: RICH

Modified 5:
TOUCH (EVERYTHING)

Open B: HAPPY

The signs in this book are easy to use once you know how. The light hands show the first position that your hands make and the dark hands show the final position. The arrows (↑ , ↓ , ↷) show which way your hand or hands move. A jagged arrow (↯) means repeat the movement. A double-headed arrow (↕) shows that your hand moves back and forth between the two positions. The squiggly marks (≈) mean that your hand touches your body. Now that you know the handshapes and the meaning of the marks, you can follow the signs in this book—and do them yourself!

Name signs are a way for deaf people to identify each other. When deaf people first meet, they fingerspell their names. But fingerspelling takes longer than signing, so deaf people have name signs. Quite often, a name sign uses the handshape of the first letter of the person's name. There are three characters in this story, King Midas, Marygold, and a soldier. King Midas's name sign has two parts—first a K handshape for *king* signed from the left shoulder to the right hip to show a royal sash, and then an M handshape for *Midas.*

KING MIDAS

Marygold is King Midas's daughter. Her name sign uses the M handshape, too, but it moves from the left shoulder to the right shoulder and then straight down to the right side of the waist. This is the sign for *princess*, except that *princess* uses the P handshape. Marygold is a princess.

The other character is a soldier. The sign for *soldier* looks like a soldier holding a rifle. This is also the sign for *army.* When we are talking about a person, many signs add an ending, called a *person marker.* The hands in an open-B shape (fingers together and palms facing), move from mid-chest level down to the waist. So by adding the person marker, the sign for *army* becomes the sign for *soldier.*

MARYGOLD SOLDIER

ASL shows time differently than English does. The story of King Midas begins, as many tales do, "once upon a time." Past tense is signaled differently in ASL than in English. Stories about the past begin with a sign near or over the shoulder. This shows "back behind" or in the past. The person signing first tells you that what he or she is talking about took place a long time ago, yesterday, or last week. Verbs do not change in ASL: *jump* and *jumped* are both signed the same, as are *sit* and *sat.* For this reason, all the ASL verbs in *King Midas* are translated into the present tense.

ONCE-UPON-A-TIME

In ASL, one sign can mean several English words, just as one English word can be translated into several different signs. Look at the sign for *put-on-robe.* This sign shows both the robe and the putting on action, the noun and the verb. The sign for *become* is used many times in this story. The same sign is used for *make, turn to,* and *change* because the same basic idea is being expressed. So sometimes when the sign for *become* is used, in English you would say *become*, and other times you would say *make, turn to,* or *change.*

PUT-ON-ROBE

BECOME
(MAKE, TURN TO, CHANGE)

TOUCH
(SOLDIER AND
KING MIDAS)

You can see from the signs below how *touch* is signed differently, depending on what is being touched. Here, one English word has several different sign variations. ASL is a "seeing" language. We can tell what is happening in the story by watching the signs.

TOUCH (EVERYTHING)

TOUCH (FLOWERS)

SIT

JUMP-INTO

GET UP

Some signs in ASL look like what they mean in English. Look at the signs for *sit, jump*, and *get up.* All three of the signs use a V handshape. Your fingers look like two legs sitting, jumping, or getting up.

This is only a short introduction to ASL. It is a beautiful language to watch and to sign. With practice, you can learn enough ASL to have a simple conversation—or tell a story.

Have fun with *King Midas* and learning some American Sign Language! The videotape that goes with this book shows a deaf actor explaining ASL and telling the story of *King Midas.* You can order the videotape or purchase it from your bookstore.

In ASL, the past tense is signaled differently than in English. Stories about the past begin with a sign showing that the action happened in the past. Verbs do not change in ASL. For this reason, all the verbs are translated into the present tense.

Once upon a time, there lived a king named Midas. King Midas was very rich. The king had a lot of gold and he loved to look at it. Every day King Midas counted his gold, and every day he wished for more.

KING
MIDAS
LOVE
MARYGOLD
MORE
THAN
GOLD.
King Midas loved Marygold more than he loved his gold.

King Midas had a beautiful young daughter named Marygold. Her beauty dazzled everyone. King Midas loved Marygold more than he loved his gold.

Marygold loved the soft, red, delicate roses in the garden. One day, she brought some roses to her father. King Midas thought, "The roses would be more beautiful if they turned to gold."

Often, King Midas rested in his garden. He daydreamed about all his gold and yearned for more.

Every afternoon, King Midas walked in his rose garden. He admired the beauty and wonderful scent of the roses, but he still wished that they would turn to gold. Often, King Midas rested in his garden. He daydreamed about all his gold and yearned for more.

KING
MIDAS
AFRAID!
TURN-
SEE
SOLDIER.
King Midas was frightened! He turned and saw a soldier.

One day, King Midas was admiring his gold. Suddenly, a bright light filled the room and a shadow appeared. King Midas was frightened! He turned and saw a soldier.

YOU
WANT
MORE
GOLD
?
"Do you want more gold?"

The soldier smiled and said, "King Midas, you are very rich. You have more gold than anyone in your country. But you always yearn for more."

"Do you want more gold?" asked the soldier.

BUT
ALWAYS
WISH
FOR
MORE.
THINK
ABOUT
GOLD
EVERY DAY.
"But I always wish for more. I think about my gold every day."

King Midas answered, "Yes, I am a very rich man, and I do have a lot of gold. But I always wish for more. I think about my gold every day."

*"King Midas, I can grant you one wish.
Think hard and tell me what you want most."*

The soldier spoke again. "King Midas, I can grant you one wish. Think hard, and tell me what you want most. But be careful what you wish!"

WISH
MAGIC
HANDS!
WANT
EVERYTHING
TOUCH
BECOME
GOLD.
"I wish for magic hands! I want everything I touch to turn to gold."

King Midas thought about his wish for a short time. Then he looked up at the soldier and smiled.

"I wish for magic hands!" said the king. "I want everything I touch to turn to gold. I will turn *everything* into gold! I will be very happy."

MAYBE
CHANGE
THINGS
BECOME
GOLD
YOU
NOT
BECOME
HAPPY.
"Maybe changing things into gold will not make you happy."

The soldier warned, "King Midas, maybe you are wrong. Maybe changing things into gold will not make you happy. Choose carefully!"

King Midas laughed and said, "No, I am right! What I desire most is more gold and still more gold! Then I will be happy!"

"Very well, King Midas, I grant you your wish," said the soldier.

SOLDIER
TOUCH
KING
TOUCH.
The soldier touched the king's hand.

he soldier touched the king's hand. A flash of brilliant light passed from the soldier to King Midas.

The soldier said, "Go to bed now, King Midas. You have your wish. Tomorrow your hands will be magic. Everything you touch will turn to gold."

The soldier disappeared.

The next morning, sunlight streamed through the window and woke King Midas.

The next morning, sunlight streamed through the window and woke King Midas. It was a beautiful day! King Midas stretched his arms and legs.

He remembered the soldier and his wish that everything he touched would turn to gold.

Suddenly, King Midas remembered! He remembered the soldier and his wish that everything he touched would turn to gold.

He picked up a book. The book became gold!

King Midas got up and put on his robe.
The cloth immediately changed to gold!

King Midas got up and put on his robe. The cloth immediately changed to gold! King Midas's wish had come true!

The king was delighted!

King Midas picked up his glasses and put them on. They turned to gold.

King Midas picked up his glasses and put them on. They turned into gold.

PULL-OPEN-HEAVY-DOOR
BECOME
GOLD.
He pulled on the heavy door and it became gold.

The king raced downstairs to go out to the rose garden. He pulled on the heavy door and it became gold.

King Midas had changed all the roses in the garden into gold with his magic hands.

The king was very excited. He ran into the rose garden and stared at the beautiful, soft, red roses. He touched a rose and it turned to gold.

Soon, King Midas had changed all the roses in the garden into gold with his magic hands.

KING
MIDAS
UPSET!
WANT
DRINK
COFFEE.
King Midas was upset! He wanted to drink the coffee.

Later, the king went into his palace for breakfast. He picked up his cup of coffee. The cup became gold! Then the *coffee* turned to gold! The hard, gold coffee fell out of the cup.

King Midas was upset! He wanted to *drink* the coffee.

NOW
ANGRY
ALSO
LITTLE-BIT
AFRAID!
Now he was angry and a little frightened!

Next, the king tried to eat pancakes. But, the pancakes became gold. King Midas was hungry.

Now he was angry and a little frightened!

LOOK,
FATHER!
HAPPEN!
FLOWER-
GROW-GROW
NOT
SOFT
RED
LIGHT
NOW.
"Look, Father! Look what happened to the roses! They are not soft and red and delicate now."

Marygold ran into the room. She was crying and holding a gold rose.

Marygold wailed, "Look, Father! Look what happened to the roses! They are not soft and red and delicate now. They are hard and yellow and ugly!"

Marygold was distressed. She cried and cried.

GIRL
BECOME
GOLD
STATUE.
KING
SHOCK!
She had become a gold statue.
The king was horrified!

King Midas reached out to comfort Marygold. She became a gold statue.

The king was horrified! He jerked back in his chair. The table and the dishes crashed to the floor.

LONG
TIME
KING
MIDAS
SIT
CRY-CRY.
For a long time, King Midas sat and cried.

For a long time, King Midas sat and cried.

Then a bright light again filled the room! The soldier appeared and stared at King Midas for a long time.

"Are you not happy? I gave you what you most desired. You have magic hands."

The soldier grasped Marygold's golden arm. He asked King Midas, "Are you not happy? I gave you what you most desired. You have magic hands. Everything you touched has turned to gold, including your precious daughter."

PLEASE
GIVE-ME
DAUGHTER
AGAIN!
"Please, I want my daughter back!"

The king answered sadly, "No, I am very unhappy."

"King Midas," the soldier asked, "do you want your *real* daughter back?"

"Oh, yes, yes, yes!" the king answered. "Please, I want my daughter back!"

BOTTLE
BRING-TO
WATER-RIVER.
JUMP-INTO
FILL-UP
WATER.
"Take this bottle to the river. Jump into the water and fill the bottle."

The soldier handed King Midas a bottle. He said, "Take this bottle to the river. Jump into the water and fill the bottle. Then pour the water on the roses. Pour the water on the food. Pour the water on Marygold."

"Everything will become real again," the soldier promised.

King Midas quickly poured water on all the gold roses. They became soft and red again.

ing Midas ran and jumped in the river. He filled the bottle with water. Then he climbed out of the river and dashed to the rose garden.

King Midas quickly poured water on all the gold roses. They became soft and red again.

The king was thrilled! He raced to the palace.

The king was even more thrilled!

King Midas poured water on the gold food that was on the floor. It became real again.

The king was even more thrilled!

MARYGOLD
BECOME
REAL
AGAIN.
KING
THRILL!
Marygold became a real girl again.
The king was delighted!

Next, the king ran to Marygold. Slowly, he poured some water on her head. Marygold became a real girl again. The king was delighted!

The soldier said, "Now you are a happy man, King Midas. Having gold is not important. You know that now."

The soldier disappeared.

King Midas had learned something important.
Gold did not make him happy.

King Midas had learned something important. The pretty roses pleased him. Good food pleased him. And, most of all, his daughter pleased him. Gold did not make him happy.

King Midas and Marygold lived in the castle for many more years. They were happy for every one of those years.

Children can learn more about sign language and deafness from the following books:

Buffy's Orange Leash, by Stephen Golder and Lise Memling, illustrated by Marcy Ramsey. Buffy, a Hearing Dog, helps the Johnson family by alerting them to sounds like the telephone and doorbell, and even when their young son Billy is crying.

ISBN 0-930323-42-4, 8½" x 7" hardcover, 32 pages, full-color illustrations

Chris Gets Ear Tubes, by Betty Pace, illustrated by Kathryn Hutton. Chris just couldn't hear right, and always he shouted "What?" when anyone spoke. This book tells what happens before, during, and after surgery for ear tubes in easy-to-understand language that will take away children's fear.

ISBN 0-930323-36-X, 7" x 9" softcover, 48 pages, full-color illustrations

The Day We Met Cindy, by Anne Marie Starowitz. In this wonderful picture storybook, a first-grade class meets Cindy, the deaf aunt of one of the students. The children's own illustrations enhance this book of learning and understanding.

ISBN 0-930323-43-2, 9" x 12" spiralbound, full-color illustrations

Discovering Sign Language, by Laura Greene and Eva B. Dicker. Children learn all about hearing loss, different sign language systems, games, and "How the Seasons Came to Be," a story in sign for elementary-age children.

ISBN 0-930323-48-3, 5¼" x 8¼" softcover, 104 pages, line drawings

I Can Sign My ABCs, by Susan Chaplin, illustrated by Laura McCaul. This full-color book has 26 signs, each with its manual alphabet handshape followed by the picture, the name, and the sign for a simple object beginning with that letter, an ideal book for teaching both the English and the American Manual alphabets.

ISBN 0-930323-19-X, 7" x 7½" hardcover, 56 pages, full-color illustrations

Little Red Riding Hood As Told in Signed English, by Harry Bornstein and Karen L. Saulnier, illustrated by Bradley O. Pomeroy. One of the most loved folktales is told through text and drawings of Signed English, the sytem that uses American Sign Language signs to give children a strong grasp of English grammar and vocabulary.

ISBN 0-930323-63-7, 8½" x 11" hardcover, 48 pages, full-color illustrations, line drawings

My First Book of Sign, Pamela J. Baker, illustrated by Patricia Bellan Gillen. This alphabet book gives the signs for the 150 words most frequently used by young children. The text includes complete explanations on how to form each sign.

ISBN 0-930323-20-3, 9" x 12" hardcover, full-color illustrations

My Signing Book of Numbers, by Patricia Bellan Gillen. Children can learn their numbers in sign language from this book, which has the appropriate number of things or creatures for numbers 0 through 20, 30, 40, 50, 60, 70, 80, 90, 100, and 1,000.

ISBN 0-930323-37-8, 9" x 12" hardcover, 56 pages, full-color illustrations

Now I Understand, by Gregory S. LaMore, illustrated by Jan Ensing-Keelan. At first, the new boy's schoolmates don't understand why he never answers their questions, and they become angry. Then, their teacher explains that he is hard of hearing, which helps the children to understand about hearing loss and "mainstreaming."

ISBN 0-930323-13-0, 5½" x 8½" flexicover, 52 pages, full-color illustrations

A Very Special Friend, by Dorothy Hoffman Levi, illustrated by Ethel Gold. Frannie, who is six, finds a very special friend. She meets Laura, who "talks" in sign language. Laura teaches Frannie signing, and they become fast friends.

ISBN 0-930323-55-6, 8½" x 7" hardcover, 32 pages, full-color illustrations